HEY, MR. ANGEL!

Christine Harder Tangvald
Illustrated by Jeff Carnehl

CPH®
SAINT LOUIS

"Hey, Mr. Angel,
Let me unhook
The top of your *halo*
From my shepherd's crook!

"I am SO SORRY.
I was running too fast.
I must have *snagged* you
As I hurried past."

"Hey, Mr. Angel,
Did you *see* all that light
And hear *trumpets blowing*
Right here in the night?

"We thought we heard *angels*
Singing so clear
That **JESUS OUR SAVIOR IS
FINALLY HERE!!**"

"Please, Mr. Angel,
What did they *say*?
We just got back—
You see, we've been away.

"We're *always* left out.
It doesn't seem fair.
What *was* it they said?
I wish we'd been there."

"There was this lamb
Who kept *running away*.
The big shepherds made **us**
Chase her **ALL DAY**.

"I finally caught her
And was lighting my lamp
When we heard this commotion
Back here at the camp."

"We heard a **LOT** of singing
And saw a bright light.
We ran back here
With all of our might.

"IS IT TRUE? IS IT TRUE?
We've waited *so long*.
What **WONDERFUL NEWS**.
What a **GLORIOUS SONG!**

"Can you please stay here
And tell us once more
About this babe Jesus
We've been *waiting for*?

"**A SAVIOR** has come,
Born, you say,
Over in Bethlehem,
Sleeping in hay?"

"In a small stable,
With a manger for a bed—
**ARE YOU REALLY SURE
THAT IS WHAT <u>GOD</u> SAID?**

"What? We can *see* **Him**—
Just look for the sign?
And in the stable,
The baby we'll find?

"There He will be—
This small **HOLY CHILD**,
With Joseph so strong
And Mary so mild?

"**OUR SAVIOR ... MY SAVIOR**
IS BORN TODAY—
GOD'S GIFT TO US
THIS CHRISTMAS DAY!"

"THANK YOU, Mr. Angel,
For this wonderful news.
I hope your halo's
Not *too bent* to use.

"Actually, Mr. Angel,
Your halo looks great.
It lost some of its glitter,
But it stands up *real straight!*"

"I'm sorry he caught you
With his shepherd's crook.
Next time he'll be
More careful to *look!*

"Now we must hurry
And catch up to the others,
With Ezra and Jacob—
They are our brothers."

"The lambs are all sleeping.
Let's hurry, let's run,
And go find the baby—
Our Savior, God's Son.

"Thank you, Mr. Angel,
For helping us find
The *way* to our Savior.
You're *especially* kind."

"GOOD-BYE, MR. ANGEL,
And THANKS once again.

Dear Parents:

Hi, there! Merry Christmas! I chose to tell the wonderful Christmas story through the dialog of two little shepherd boys so your child can be right there—with them—witnessing and experiencing the story as it happens. Looking through the eyes of the small shepherd boys, your child will experience the excitement of hearing the **GOOD NEWS** *of the birth of the Christ Child— told by a* **REAL ANGEL.**

I hope you will enjoy the bouncy, lyrical verse. Laugh together and shout "Hurray!" as you read and celebrate the birth of your Savior.

Much love and God bless!

Christine